Best
Worst
Ever

L.D. BLAKELEY

BEST WORST EVER
2nd Edition © 2017 L.D. Blakeley

ISBN-13: 978-0-9959750-0-2

1st Edition © 2014 L.D. Blakeley
1st edition published digitally as part of the 2014
Dreamspinner Press *Daily Dose*.

www.ldblakeley.com

Editor: Melanie Fletcher

Cover Artist: Lisa Trainor-diNorcia

DEDICATION

To Alex, my Happily Ever After.

CONTENTS

ACKNOWLEDGMENTS

Thanks to my husband, Alex, for his unwavering support
and general rockstarriness (it's a word!)
I owe huge kudos to my editor/critique/beta reader
extraordinaire, Melanie Fletcher.
And I'd also like to thank the good folks at
Dreamspinner Press who took a chance on an unknown
author and published the original version of this story.

CHAPTER ONE

"MAKE SURE that organza doesn't catch on the edge of the table, Andrew. And watch that the seams are facing in!" Not that Carey thought, for a second, his second-in-command would ever make such a rookie mistake. But the past three months had been hellish and he was reaching the end of his tether. Without even a weekend's relief from the mad preholiday scramble, he was more than ready for a break, even if he didn't see one happening anytime soon. Each year got busier than the last, but this season seemed to have taken him and his small staff of party planners by surprise. To say that his edges were beginning to frazzle was a bit of an understatement.

A flurry of bodies and voices fought for supremacy in the cramped party room. Despite the fact that his current client's last-minute requests were getting more and more ridiculous and more and more last minute, Carey kept his cool and smiled politely at the Demon Diva (as he'd fondly named her in his head) currently tapping an over-the-top acrylic manicure against an equally over-the-top rhinestone belt. After all, she was a client. And as such, she was paying a generous fee to have Carey's team "sort out all the drama," as she had charmingly put it during their first meeting. *But, seriously, who changes a party's entire color scheme to accommodate a new hairstyle that "just totally spoke to me"?*

Logan Carey English, owner and sole proprietor of Carey's Catering & Events, did a mean business with his quirky band of misfits. He'd started the company as part of a marketing project during his last year at university. He had only meant to create a fictitious enterprise for the purposes of building a business and PR plan, but his professor had bragged it up at a mixer one night in the presence of the Dean's wife, who couldn't resist pouncing on a cheap source of labor. And after having done all the necessary legwork and planning for her fundraiser, word spread. More and more people with cash-lined pockets came knocking on his door, and he realized pretty quickly that his passion wasn't going to be in selling products for a corporate fat cat. In fact, he hated the idea. What he liked was seeing people happy. And, with the rare tragic exception, helping people throw their dream parties or weddings pretty much fit that bill to a T.

The sudden chirp of his cell phone had Carey wishing he could escape, however—even if just for a moment—from the hustle of his world. *An isolated island with no technology and no clients or staff. Wouldn't that just be a slice of heaven?* Not that he'd seriously consider giving up what he'd created. Despite its accidental inception, Carey's Catering & Events had been a lot of years in the making. He'd put every bit of his money, time, and considerable effort into building something he could call his own and do so with pride.

"I'm so sorry, I have to take this," he apologized to his client, then added, "Andrew, could you please come help Miss Masters choose a different color gel for her up-lighting that won't clash with her lovely new highlights?" *Demon Diva, indeed*, he chuckled to himself.

"I owe you," he whispered as his flamboyant assistant scrambled to his rescue.

"Promises, promises," Andrew sighed dramatically as he turned to the Demon Diva.

Carey slipped around a corner and quickly answered the call. "Carey's Catering and Events, Carey speaking."

"Who you making promises to now, Logan?"

Carey grinned, though his pulse stuttered ever-so-slightly. Only one person ever called him by his first name—partly to do with an affinity for *X-Men,* but primarily to tease. Only one person could consistently make his heart race without trying and turn his cock to granite with just the sound of his voice. Unfortunately, he also happened to be the one man Carey knew better than to think of that way. Unfortunately, logic didn't always stop his traitorous mind from an occasional trip down that particular X-rated rabbit hole.

Carey and Darcy Skyler Wood had been friends since their freshman year at university when fate saw fit to place them across the hall from each other in the same residence. It never mattered to Sky that Carey was gay. Nor did it matter to Carey that Sky wasn't. They simply clicked. A shared love of bad science fiction, cheesy horror movies, and gooey, greasy pizza had made them fast friends. So, when they fell into a pattern of sharing more evenings together than not, Carey figured he could hardly be blamed for developing feelings for his handsome—albeit straight—friend. Not that he'd ever acted on said feelings. Not in four years of college or any of the years that followed. But that hadn't made any difference to the torch that seemed to continue on a low and steady burn.

"Merry Christmas, Mr. Darcy! To what do I owe the pleasure?" Carey knew he was the only one who could get away with the nickname and took great pleasure in using it whenever possible.

"Lord Logan of English," Sky teased, in a deplorable attempt at a British accent. "Did I catch you at a bad time?"

Damn. His voice could still do that voodoo, crap accent be damned.

"Not at all—just in the middle of a fiber-optics fiasco. I've got Andrew handling it."

"Is that *all* Andrew's handling?" Sky chuckled in a way that, to Carey, always fell somewhere between lewd and lovely.

"What? No! God, Sky. Drew works for me. Besides, even if I were so inclined, I'm a little long in the tooth to be competing with the constant circling of young twinks in his orbit."

In fairness, thirty-two wasn't exactly ready to be put out to pasture. But compared to the stream of barely twentysomethings always at Andrew's heel, it seemed downright ancient. And when he stopped for a second to consider the state of his own social life, or lack thereof, Carey felt... old. He spent long days working with clients, suppliers, and his small but loyal team. And when he wasn't working on a specific event, he was busy attending trade shows and researching the latest trends. Because if there was one thing he knew for certain, it was that people willing to pay someone else to throw their party liked to show off the trendiest of things—no matter how ridiculous those trends might be.

He didn't mind though. Truth be told, he preferred barely having a moment to himself. He'd rather be busy making other people smile than left alone for too long with his thoughts. That only led to introspection. And Lord knows, he didn't need that. When was the last time he'd actually gone on a date? Oh, right. Stephen. No need to dwell there.

"What's up?" he asked. No matter how tight his schedule, he always made time for Sky. "I haven't heard from you in weeks. Figured you'd chucked all my wedding planning and eloped somewhere tropical."

"No. No eloping. No wedding, actually." The hitch in Sky's voice was almost imperceptible. It might have gone unnoticed had he been talking to anyone other than Carey.

"Wait—what do you mean, no wedding? I thought you and Elise had set a date. June twenty-seventh, right? I've got you slated in with high priority that weekend. All the VIP bells and whistles." Not that he particularly relished seeing Sky swear his undying love for someone else before friends, family, and whatever deity might be watching down from on high. But this was his best friend for whom he'd do pretty much anything, including plan his wedding, if that's what was going to make Sky happy. His best friend who he'd seen go through no less than a half dozen breakups with long-term girlfriends over the years, each one seeming to dull the light in Sky's eyes just a bit further.

"Sky? What aren't you telling me? What happened?"

"Elise left. She just—" Sky's voice sounded shaky and unsure. "There's not going to be any wedding. I know the deposit is yours, and that's fine. But—"

"I don't give a shit about the deposit, Sky. Jesus. Are … are you okay?"

"I'll be fine. She's not the first one to leave. I'm sure she won't be the last."

"She's the first one you were going to marry, Sky. Don't act stoic on my account. We've known each other way too long for that."

"I know. It's just…" The sentence faded into a sigh.

"Just nothing. Where are you right now?" Carey knew there couldn't be a worse time to think about dropping everything to run to Sky's rescue. But that's exactly what he was contemplating.

"I'm in the city. At the condo. But I have that

big, fancy chalet-cottage thing up in Blue Mountain that I rented for New Years. So I'll likely head there the day before New Year's Eve. We were going to spend Christmas with her family," he continued quietly. "This was supposed to be our first getaway as almost marrieds. How pathetic is that?"

"It's not pathetic, Sky. It's unfortunate, and it sucks. But it's not pathetic." Carey hated hearing sorrow in Sky's voice. It wasn't an emotion Sky often expressed, so it packed a wallop when it did surface.

"All you have to do is cancel and get a refund," Carey offered. "We'll go someplace warm with cold drinks and hot babes—pretty boys and girls in bikinis as far as the eye can see!" He was prepared to do whatever it took to cheer up his heartbroken friend.

"We?"

"Yes, we. You don't think I'm going to let you be alone right now to wallow, do you? Besides, you can't ring in the New Year alone. I'm pretty sure it's illegal. I know it's unconscionable."

"Unconscionable? That's a pretty big word, Carey. You got a word-of-the day calendar?"

"Whatever. And shut up. My point is, it's not happening. Not on my watch, buddy."

"Thanks, Care, but I can't ask you to do that— not at your busiest time of year. Besides, I can't get a refund." The dejection in Sky's voice nearly broke Carey's heart. "I already tried."

"Then we'll celebrate in the snow. We'll get fall-down, stupid drunk, eat disgusting junk food, watch terrible movies, and talk smack about all our exes. Lord knows I've got some spectacular fuck-ups worth sharing. It'll be fabulous!" He hoped the faux enthusiasm he was pumping into his voice sounded legit. "Just as long as I don't have to actually go out in the snow. This place has indoor plumbing, right? And electricity?" Not usually prone to affectation, Carey knew how mincing he sounded. But he'd play it up to the nines if it meant he could put some semblance of a smile back onto Sky's face.

The almost chuckle he'd elicited from his friend only solidified for Carey that he had no choice but to leave his team in charge and take a break, take time out and be there for Sky. They were more than capable of handling things without him for a few days. And besides, it wasn't like he had a date—or any plans at all, for that matter—on New Year's Eve.

"Yes, it has indoor plumbing. A hot tub, even. If you play your cards right, you might be able to sweet talk me into it." The teasing in Sky's voice left no doubt that his comment was in jest. It didn't, however, stop a jolt of heat from rolling through Carey as he pictured how that might play out. *You do enjoy torturing yourself, don't you, English?*

"Smart ass." Carey chuckled. "Text me the details, Sky, and I'll make plans to be your New Year's Knight in Shining Armor."

"My hero," Sky deadpanned.

"Do you want to come for Christmas at Mom's? I know she'd love to see you. I'll be here, in the city, tonight and tomorrow. But I was planning to drive up to St. Jacobs Christmas morning and spend a few days there."

Carey's mom had lived in Toronto, where she'd worked as a travel agent for years. But when online booking agents began muscling out smaller, independent agencies, she took it as a sign to embrace early retirement. Since she preferred a quieter, simpler existence, she packed up, moved to the tiny touristy village, and never looked back. *Never cared much for the rat race anyway*, she'd joked. *Might as well live someplace pretty.* He couldn't argue with her there.

"Nah. Thanks, though. I think I'd rather have a few days to—what did you call it? Wallow?" An uneasy sigh turned into a chuckle. "Besides, I've already let too many of my staff take extended holidays this year. I need to be available in case anything comes up."

Carey knew Sky's job as administrator for one of the city's largest nursing homes was one that took up a lot of time. That didn't stop Carey from asking though.

"Are you sure? You know she'll have enough food for an entire team of football players. And enough wine for a full squad of soccer moms." He wanted to force the issue, but Sky's tone wasn't completely dire, and was enough to keep Carey from worrying too much about leaving his friend alone for part of the holidays. *At least it's only a few days.*

"But maybe just save me a soccer mom?"

"Done and done."

"Talk soon, English." Sky paused, and Carey could swear he heard wheels spinning in overdrive. "Carey? You know you really are… Just, thanks. Thanks, man."

"My pleasure, Sky."

L.D. BLAKELEY

CHAPTER TWO

"CARE BEAR—just go. I promise, we've got this. You've done all the planning and prep, doll. Everything will be fine. Plus you've got the most amazing team of worker bees in the world. We'll make sure everything is fabulous, and you'll look like a god. Now go and help that handsome man mend a broken heart and ring in the New Year with a bang. Or a high five, or whatever it is straight boys do when the clock strikes midnight."

Contrary to outward appearances, Andrew was anything but the dizzy queen he often portrayed. He'd been a fixture at Carey's almost since the beginning and had seen Carey through more than one disastrous dating endeavor. So Carey was fairly certain Andrew knew his feelings toward

Sky weren't entirely platonic.

But were they unrequited? Most definitely.

"High five?" Carey asked with a quizzical grin.

Andrew flipped his hands in dismissal. "Well, how should I know? Just go. Go and pray for good weather. Or at least until you get there. Then pray for pretty ski bunnies—both flavors. A good roll in a snow bank would do you good too, mister."

Carey feigned outrage and playfully slapped Andrew on the shoulder. "Thanks, Drew. I really do owe you."

"Yes, yes you do. Now go! Spend Christmas Day with your mom, doing Christmassy things."

That boy just earned himself a healthy year-end bonus.

Carey already had his car packed and ready to go. The weather seemed to be holding up and, thankfully, St. Jacobs wasn't far from Toronto. He'd be able to make it there in less than two hours, assuming traffic didn't bottleneck along the 401. Frustratingly, the longest part of the drive would be getting from his downtown condo to the city outskirts. *Ah well. The pros and cons of city life.*

Christmas with his mom had never been the Ozzy and Harriet production that so many families tried to replicate. Granted, the absence of any "Ozzy" from the picture sort of eliminated them from the running right from the get-go.

Carey didn't know his father. The coward had hightailed it as soon as the rabbit died. But that never stopped his mom from doing everything in her power to ensure Carey always had a Christmas worth remembering. And, truth be told, Carey much preferred their quirky Christmas celebrations to the starched and scratchy ordeals he'd heard so many of his friends describe.

Despite all efforts to celebrate against the grain, his mom held hard and fast to one holiday tradition that never failed to bring a smile to Carey's face. And, as he pulled into his mother's driveway, he could see that this year she'd pulled out all the stops. Her modest, cottage-like house was decked out in more lights than he'd thought possible. He knew she'd have hauled the ladder around and affixed each one herself, too. Every conceivable inch of the small gable front was covered in lights of all shapes and sizes, making it twinkle like a storybook gingerbread house. Any notion of a Mrs. Claus residing within, however, were dispelled with the statuesque raven- haired Stevie Nicks clone who barreled out the front door as he put the car in park.

"Prince Charming! You made it!" His mother's nickname might have made him roll his eyes, but it always made him feel loved. She'd told him not long after he'd come out that there was no need to wait around for Prince Charming to appear and sweep him off his feet. That was too obvious, she'd explained. He was a better man than that and worthy of being the charming prince, himself. He'd yet to live up to that sweeping potential, though he had tried.

"Jeez, Mom—did Clark Griswold help you decorate?" The house was well past the realms of gaudy this year, and he expected nothing less from his delightfully unconventional mother. She simply didn't do boring.

"Don't you sass your Momma." A fake southern drawl was punctuated with a warm rumbling laugh.

"Merry Christmas, Ms. Dubois. Did you rely on the kindness of strangers to help with all of this?" He gestured toward the house, already knowing how she would answer.

"Now why would I have someone else interfere with my artistic vision?" Isabel English grinned widely and grabbed her only child in a crushing bear hug.

The next few days of food, rest and all-around general sloth flew by far more quickly than Carey would have imagined. But at least his overworked and utterly exhausted self had a chance to recharge and mend the burned-out brain cells he knew were bound to start causing problems sooner rather than later. He felt a quiet peace his daily routine didn't often allow. It was nice. Until he started to think about Sky, that is. Then all bets were off as he started to fret about being in such close quarters with the object of his unwelcome fantasies. Nevertheless, he knew his friend needed him. *Cowboy up, English. You can do this.*

The night before Carey was set to head up to Blue Mountain and join Sky, he sat peacefully with his mother in front of a crackling fireplace as they enjoyed a deliciously smooth eighteen-year-old single malt.

"What happened with you and Stephen, honey?" His mother casually topped up the Glencairn glasses he'd given to her as part of this year's Christmas gift.

"Right to the point, eh, Mom?" He knew that trying to deflect the conversation would be futile. It didn't keep him from slowly sipping the proffered drink to delay responding.

"Well, you seemed so happy when he was around."

"Yeah, but he hasn't been around for a long time, Mom. We weren't even officially, you know, together. He couldn't…" Carey sighed heavily and set his drink down. "Let's just say that the view from his closet was extremely limited."

"He certainly made no pretense about the nature of your relationship when I was around. He seemed so forthright and charming the last time the two of you visited."

"Because he knew he could be. You weren't ever going to cross paths with anyone else in his world."

"Did you love him?"

"I don't know. I thought I did. It doesn't matter, anyway. Obviously, I wasn't worth fighting for. Because when I called him on it, he opted to walk away rather than live an honest life." He considered the rich amber liquor in his glass. "I'm not sure I did, though. Love him." Although it had felt real enough at the time.

Isabel cocked her head and tucked an errant lock of hair behind one ear. "I think it might be time for you to adjust your yardstick, honey."

"What's that supposed to mean?"

"Don't play coy, Prince Charming. It doesn't become you." She stretched and smiled. "I think maybe you need to stop giving your heart to unavailable men. I think maybe you need to stop measuring every man you meet against your handsome Mr. Darcy."

"That's ridiculous. I don't do any such thing." He knew he was lying before the words left his mouth. He did *exactly* such a thing. But he sure as hell wasn't going to admit it aloud. Because that would be nothing short of folly. It was one thing to feel something and try like hell to ignore it. It was something else, entirely, to put words to it and let it out into the universe. That would make it real. And that would well and truly crush him.

"If you say so, honey." But the look on her face was anything but placated. Carey's mom leaned slowly forward, her armful of bangles chiming delicately. "So ... what are your plans for New Year's?"

Oh. She was good.

CHAPTER THREE

DESPITE BEING directionally challenged, Carey had faith in technology and diligently followed the prompts doled out by his GPS. *This can't be it*, he thought as he pulled up to a charming, picturesque cabin.

If there was one thing he knew about Sky, it was that he was as frugal as the day was long. And, judging by the other places he'd passed along the way, he was guessing the impressive exterior of this place matched a rather swanky, if not romantic, interior. *Of course, idiot. Sky had rented the place thinking he'd be with his fiancée. Not his best friend.*

He parked next to his friend's SUV and stubbornly grabbed more than he could carry at once. Why make two trips when you can do it in one? Necessity might be the mother of invention, but laziness was definitely its big, bad daddy. Laden down with a suitcase and far too many bags of food and liquor, Carey used the toe of his boot to gently knock at the front door. "Sky? You in there? My hands are full, man, come open the door." When there was no response, he tried again with the tip of his boot. "Mr. Darcy, are—"

His sentence was cut short as the door flew open. "Jesus! Hold your horses, Logan. I couldn't hear you with the water running. I was just in the…"

Shower. He'd been in the shower. Carey knew this, not because he suddenly had the ability to read minds. Oh, no. He knew this because there, in front of him, stood all six foot four inches of Darcy Skyler Wood … dripping wet with nothing but a towel slung low around his hips. *Shit.*

Don't stare. Don't stare at that solitary drop of water as it slowly slides its way between the hard, flat planes of those perfect pecs. And for the love of all that's holy, do not stare *at anything even remotely near the edge of that towel!* But Carey never was any good at taking orders.

"Here. Make yourself useful and take a few of these bags," Carey all but barked, pushing his way past the man he was *not* staring at and making his way through the front door.

"Hey! Broken-hearted man here. Where's my

hug?" Sky opened his arms wide and grinned idiotically.

"Put some pants on, and we'll discuss."

"I'm guessing that's the exact opposite of what you'd normally say to a man in this state of dress?" Sky's raised eyebrow and hip shimmy weren't meant to captivate. Too bad they did anyway.

"Smart ass. Go get dressed, and I'll fix some drinks." When Sky headed back to what Carey assumed was a bedroom, he heaved a sigh of relief and set about hauling in the rest of his provisions.

After one more mule-headed trip to the car, Carey finally had everything in and unpacked. And, with two strong whiskys in hand, he joined his now fully dressed friend in the living room.

"How's Isabel?" Sky sat back on the sofa and propped two long legs up on the coffee table, crossing them at the ankle.

"Very Isabel." Carey handed over one of the drinks and sat next to Sky with one leg tucked under the opposite knee.

"Let me guess. She plied you with good scotch and grilled you about your love life."

"Doesn't she always?" Carey snickered, knowing full well the fodder he created with his attempts and failures at relationships.

"At least you know her heart is always in the

right place."

"Yeah. That's true. But she doesn't have to be so damn astute all the time." He knocked back the rest of his drink in an attempt to drown out his mother's words. A few more at this pace and he wouldn't understand words, period. "So do you want to talk about what happened with Elise?" No point dancing around the big, fat, brokenhearted elephant in the room.

"She said she couldn't do it anymore. Said life was too short, and she didn't want to be wasting any more time. Said she couldn't compete. So she broke it off."

"Couldn't compete?" Carey's mind raced, trying to put two and two together. "Shit, Sky. Did you have an affair?" It seemed so outside the realm of possibility, but he had to ask. Sky wasn't the type to cheat. Was he?

His friend glared at him. "No, I'm not having an affair! What the fuck, man?"

"Sorry. I don't know why I asked that. But you're being all vague and cryptic."

"I want to drink." Sky's tone and taciturn expression implied that the topic was no longer up for discussion.

"Then drink we shall." Carey was willing to play both bartender and court jester.

Two hours, an entire bottle of Glenlivet, and a host of good-natured ribbing and bad jokes seemed to have smoothed over any feathers that might have been ruffled at the mention of infidelity.

"Remember that trip we took second year to see the petroglyphs?" Sky had sprawled into a boneless pile of limbs across most of the sofa. His feet were now tucked under Carey's hip, and his toes were rhythmically tapping to the beat of some unknown song playing in his head.

"You mean the trip where you picked up the girl in the gift shop and left without telling us where you went?"

Sky chuckled. "She wanted you, you know."

"What? She did not."

"She did. I noticed it right away. She watched you from the minute we walked through the door. When the rest of our group was finished, I saw her head in your direction and I headed her off at the pass."

"You're all heart," Carey laughed. "Did you tell her she wasn't my type? Or did you just dazzle her with your patented Skyler Wood charm?"

"Both." Sky grinned lazily. The potent whisky had clearly worked its warm and toasty magic.

"She asked if we'd ever … y'know. Said she'd have paid good money to see that."

"Good Christ." Carey laughed uncomfortably.
I'd have paid more.

"D'ya ever think about it, though?"

"Think about what?" *Play dumb. Play dumb.*

"Me and you?"

"Wha'? Of course not!" *Damn. That came out a bit sharper than anticipated.*

"My rippling biceps and sweet, sweet ass not up to your standards?" Sky slurred.

Carey snorted. Actually snorted. "We're friends, moron. Also? There's the small matter of you being straight." The grin on his face was forced. He knew this was a line of questioning that could go nowhere good. *Kill it. Kill it with fire!*

But he needn't have worried. Because the next thing he heard from his friend was the faint snuffle of snoring. He grabbed the blanket from the back of the sofa and threw it over his unconscious friend, lightly ghosting the tips of his fingers across the soft hair that had fallen across Sky's face.

"Good night, Mr. Darcy."

SLOW, WET heat enveloped him completely. He arched into the touch, slowly and steadily fucking the mouth wrapped around his rigid cock. "Fuck, yes … that's it." Raking his fingers through dark curls, Carey held his lover's head in place and continued his rhythmic thrusts. His lover hummed happily, sending a crackle of electricity through his dick and straight into his balls. "Ahh… Yes! Please." He knew he wouldn't last. Not at this pace. Not with those clever fingers tracing hot circles around his asshole. Just as he thought he'd reached the precipice, that exquisite mouth pulled slowly off his cock with a deliciously filthy-sounding pop. With a whimper, he forced his lover back where he wanted him most. But instead of sucking him in, those full, sumptuous lips teased the head of his dick mercilessly. Tiny, darting licks around the rim had him writhing and babbling, begging for more. The teasing was torturous. But before he could form the words to beg, he felt an index finger breach his inner ring as his cock was swallowed to the root. Feeling his world shrink to exclude everything but his cock and the sensations being created around it by that talented mouth, Carey shivered and moaned as he writhed uncontrollably. "OhmygodSky!" he rasped in one sucking breath.

FUCK.

So much for sleep. Wide awake and hard as a rock, Carey scrubbed his hands across his face and through his hair, then stared silently up at the ceiling, praying for Morpheus to kick his ass into oblivion for the rest of the night.

L.D. BLAKELEY

CHAPTER FOUR

CAREY WASN'T sure when he drifted off again. Mercifully, the Sandman did creep in at some point during the night. Unfortunately, the mincing magical bastard thought it would be cute to leave behind the fucking Kodo Drummers, who were currently beating a skull-splitting wake-up call through his head. *Scotch strikes again.*

A flash of last night's conversation filtered into his brain, and he seriously contemplated rolling back over to sleep away the entire morning. But a haze of sunlight dancing through the gap in the bedroom curtains and the smell of coffee was enough to tempt him back to the land of the living.

Sky was busy fixing pancakes when Carey finally managed to drag himself upright to forage for caffeine. He stood at the stove, with his back to the rest of the kitchen, affording Carey the opportunity to simply … look.

Sky's was a long, lanky beauty: broad shoulders, narrow waist, a mop of hair the color of brown sugar, and a slightly crooked grin that turned Carey to mush. His low-slung jeans allowed the slightest hint of the glorious curve of his ass and long, muscular legs. But what really cut through the fog of Carey's hangover was the smattering of dark-golden hair and freckles that dusted Sky's lean, sculpted torso.

Shirtless. He has to be standing there shirtless.

Carey discreetly adjusted himself and poured a cup of strong, black coffee.

Trying hard to ignore the state of dress—or undress, as was more the case—currently assaulting his senses, Carey attempted levity as the quickest path of avoidance. "Why, Mr. Darcy. You cook?"

"What am I, some kind of savage?" Sky arched an eyebrow and handed Carey a plate of fluffy, golden pancakes, then gestured toward the table. "There are still a few things you don't know about me."

"No, I just remember a few of your more outstanding failed attempts back in university. YouTube lessons?"

"Fuck off," Sky said with a grin, sitting down

with his own plate of pancakes. "Besides, I've learned lots of things from the internet. I've got skills that would shiver your timbers, matey." Said through a giant mouthful of breakfast, it should have sounded ridiculous. Unfortunately, it led Carey's mind to all sorts of inappropriate places. *Of that I have no doubt, Mr. Darcy. No doubt whatsoever.*

"Avast, Sir Logan, with what shall we while away the hours today, me lad?"

"Well, if you keep talking like a pirate, I'm going to finish my pancakes and coffee and go back to bed."

"I'll have you know this is the 'My Fiancée Dumped Me And I Have Nobody To Kiss At Midnight' New Year's Extravaganza. Arrr! Don't hate on the pirate speak, dude."

Carey could only shake his head and smile. He had to hand it to Sky. Nobody seemed to take a breakup quite like he did. He never got maudlin. He never seemed to feel sorry for himself. He never fell apart. He simply took the hand he'd been dealt and got right back into the game. Throw in affable charm, sparkling hazel bedroom eyes, and a smile that could melt the polar icecaps, and it was no surprise that there was always another young lovely quick to step into the shoes of the recently departed.

"Okay, then, Mr. 'It's My Party And I'll Act A

Tool If I Want To.' The day is yours. What tickles your fancy?"

Sky placed the fork he'd been wielding like a sabre on the edge of his plate and contemplated the question, pursing his lips as though in deep thought. The carefully arched eyebrow let Carey know that any forthcoming suggestions were bound to land somewhere between the realms of utterly ridiculous and completely absurd. Sky did not disappoint.

"Naked snow angels?"

"I'm thinking no."

"Naked tobogganing?"

"Again with the no."

"Naked snowman-building contest?"

"See, now maybe I don't really know when it comes to straight guys. But I have to say that as a gay man—and I'm pretty sure I'm safe in speaking on behalf of gay men everywhere—I have *way* more respect for my junk than to go humping it into a snow bank."

"So … what will you hump it into, then?"

Careful, English.

"Well, judging by my less than stellar track record, I'd have to venture, anyone who says 'yes'?" It wasn't that Carey was completely unable to attract men. The main problem had always been his inability to keep one. Or, rather, keep one publicly or exclusively. He knew that, empirically speaking, he wasn't ugly. At five foot nine, he might not have been blessed with the "tall" factor in the Tall, Dark, and Handsome equation. But the thick, dark hair he'd inherited from his mother and the strong jawline and sharp cheekbones, presumably from his father, combined agreeably in a way that—sadly for Carey—seemed to attract more single women than out-and-proud gay men. And when he was fortunate enough to attract the right gender, it was usually in the form of an out-and-out player, or an in-and-in closet case.

"Naked Twister?" Sky suggested.

Jesus. There's a visual.

"I'm not sure I'm all that bendy."

"Don't sell yourself short." Sky snickered, then continued, "Naked charades?"

"If you were to maybe suggest something involving a bit more clothing, I might be inclined to say yes, you know."

"Since when do you turn down random acts of nudity from recently single and emotionally vulnerable men? I mean, jeez. I'm obviously distraught and in need of comfort." Sky batted his eyes like a bad sketch-comedy version of Scarlett O'Hara.

"Since said offers are coming from an ever-so-straight and full-of-shit asshat of a man with more maple syrup on his elbow than on his pancakes."

The oven mitt that hit Carey square in the face wasn't a complete surprise. Better that than the iron skillet.

CHAPTER FIVE

A LAZY morning-to-afternoon movie marathon of *Hot Fuzz, Shaun of the Dead*, and *The World's End* seemed to be just the ticket to happiness—especially since the snow that had started that morning was now falling in heavy, wet flakes. The idea of facing all that cold mess, naked or otherwise, left both men perfectly content with their choice of sloth.

A couple of medium-rare steaks and a mountain of garlic mashed potatoes for dinner hadn't detracted from the current state of lethargy, either. It might not have been the most scintillating New Year's Eve celebration in the world, but neither man seemed inclined to complain.

"I need alcohol." Sky stretched his long, lean

frame across the sofa and teasingly poked at Carey with his big toe.

Carey shot a look over his shoulder from his spot on the floor. "What, two six-packs of beer aren't enough for you? And keep your toes to yourself, buddy."

"Hey, I shared! And you love my toes. Admit it. You can't get enough of my toes." With a gleeful and slightly sinister expression on his face, Sky sat up and dug both feet into Carey's ribs.

"Gah! You tool! Get off!" Carey instinctively grabbed at the offending appendages in question and pulled them away from his extremely ticklish sides. Not one to be bested, he quickly gained purchase around Sky's ankles and yanked him off the edge of the couch. Using his long legs to his advantage, however, Sky was quick to wrap Carey in a sad attempt at a wrestling hold and flip him, unceremoniously, onto his back.

"I think you bit off more than you can chew with, earth mate." Sky had Carey pinned beneath him, laughing, their faces only inches apart.

"Don't quote Simon Pegg at me, you clown." Despite the disconcerting jolt of lust he felt from their nearness, Carey couldn't help but smile up at Sky. "Get off me, you oaf, and I'll fix the first round." Sky didn't move right away. And part of Carey was tempted to simply enjoy the electric hum that was starting to vibrate through his body. Common sense stepped up, however. And rather than torture himself further, Carey shoved Sky to the side and rolled to his feet, praying the erection he was now sporting was hidden from view. "How do whisky sours sound?" he asked as he strolled off to the kitchen in a manner he hoped looked casual and unaffected.

"Tonight, we will be partaking of a liquid repast!" Sky's British accent truly was horrible.

The heavy snow and whipping wind outside the kitchen window made Carey grateful to be tucked away inside with heat, electricity, and drinks. *Definitely the drinks.* He'd had years to temper the lust he felt for Sky. He *knew* it was ridiculous. Besides, he was supposed to be providing a shoulder right now, not any other eager body part that felt it could play a part in the weekend. But it wasn't even so much the more obvious appendage he was concerned with.

Carey had shielded his heart for so long, keeping his lovers at arm's length. At first, he wasn't aware that he did so. He'd only meant to keep a solid and distinct line between loving his best friend and *loving* him. Unfortunately, that reserve had done him no favors in the long run. As a result, he'd never let anyone else in, either. Never let anyone get close. Never allowed himself to really feel. Although he had come close with Stephen, close to opening himself up and letting himself fall. In retrospect, that stoic detachment had served him well, he guessed, at least in that particular case. It wasn't that he needed, or expected, grand gestures or flowery proclamations. And he knew that Stephen had cared for him. Just not enough.

So, yeah. Drinks. The stronger, the better.

Carey girded his resolve and headed back to the living room, two glasses and a very powerful pitcher of whisky sours in hand.

"Okay, Sir Toes-a-Lot, I have us a full pitcher of—" The sentence was abruptly cut off as the cabin was thrown into darkness. *What was that about a break from technology? Careful what you wish for.*

"Oh, shit," Sky muttered. "They warned that the power could go out if a bad enough storm hit."

"Do you have a lighter?" Carey gingerly felt his way across the room and set the drinks down before they could add cleaning in the dark to their New Year's Eve festivities.

"Yeah, hang on. We should be good. I think there are a bunch of candles over in the cabinet by the fireplace. And the window seat has a storage shelf underneath that's full of wood to burn. I just need some paper of something for kindling."

Sky rummaged around until he found the candles, lit several, and then set about ensuring a source of heat. Carey let his eyes adjust to the dim glow of light and watched quietly as Sky knelt in front of the fireplace and worked on building a fire. *Jesus, he's beautiful. I couldn't have an ugly best friend?* But he knew better, knew that wouldn't have made any difference.

"And we have fire!" Sky proclaimed, proudly, hands on hips in a superhero stance.

"My hero." Carey's dry delivery was somewhat tempered by the goofy grin on his face. "So much for the movie marathon-ing, though. Good thing I stocked in enough liquor for a fleet."

"Carey, you trollop, did you invite sailors to my New Year's Eve Pity Party?"

"If I had, do you think I'd be wasting this perfectly good blackout on you?" Carey waggled his eyebrows.

Sky flopped dramatically to the floor and poured two hearty-sized drinks. "You don't love me anymore."

"Oh, Skyler. I'll always love you." And wasn't that just the slap-you-in-the-face truth?

"Besides, everyone knows sailors are good on water. And we're on land. Who would build you a fire? How would you stay warm?"

"Well, you see, Sky—when a sailor boy and a gay boy really, really like each other…" He let the rest trail off and grinned.

Sky took a huge swallow of his drink, then

glared amusedly at Carey. "Smart ass."

"All this talk of sailors and my ass is making we wish I had brought a date." Carey was only half kidding.

"You never did tell me what happened with Stephen."

"Nothing." Carey swigged his drink and continued. "Nothing big or dramatic, anyway. I wanted us to be together and so did he. He just didn't want anyone to know about it. And my closet was too small when I was sixteen, so I sure as hell wasn't about to step back in. Not for him. Not for any man."

"Did you love him?"

If anyone had asked him at the time, he would have said yes. He'd always just assumed that he had. But if that were the case, would he have been so quick to let things end?

"I … I'm not sure that I did."

"I'm sorry, Care. That sucks."

"Yeah, well. One day, Matthew McConaughey will decide he plays for the wrong team, show up at my door in a cowboy hat and chaps, and all my prayers will be answered." Carey laughed and continued, "Are failed love affairs really what you want to be talking about, though, right now?"

"Talking about someone else's distracts me from thinking about my own."

"I'm so glad my failed relationships can serve

some greater purpose." Carey refilled their glasses to the brim and handed one back to Sky. "Cheers, then, my friend. Here's to us talking about things that make you smile and to getting boiled-as-an-owl drunk!"

Sky raised his glass before quaffing back a mouthful. "Cheers to that! And to another of what I can only assume is one of your mother's colorful expressions."

"She is nothing, if not colorful." Carey knew he was lucky to have such a free-spirited strong woman in his life. The way she had raised him was part of the reason he was able to stand up to Stephen and issue him an ultimatum. Granted, he didn't get the outcome he'd hoped for, but such was often the case with throwing down those sorts of gauntlets.

"Did you ever go to summer camp when you were a kid?" Sky finished the rest of his drink and was filling their glasses, yet again.

"No, why? Is that where you learned to knock these back like Kool-Aid?" He held his glass aloft, shaking it to clink the ice.

"Funny. No, but we did learn to amuse ourselves in the dark."

"Why, Mr. Darcy. I do declare! This sounds downright scandalous!" Carey's fake southern accent was only marginally better than Sky's attempt at sounding British.

"Ha-ha. Camp games, you dirty bastard. We can play Truth or Dare while we wait for the power to come back!" Sky sounded far too eager. Carey felt queasy.

"What are you, a nine-year-old girl? I'm not playing Truth or Dare."

"Okay, then. We'll play Best Worst Ever."

"That all depends on one thing. What the hell is Best Worst Ever?"

Sky ran into the kitchen to refill their now-depleted pitcher of drinks, all the while yelling back to Carey. "Only the best game ever!"

"I was right. You are a nine-year-old girl," Carey teased.

"Fuck you, Logan. It's my party, and we're playing."

"Oh good, guilt. My favorite."

"It goes well with alcohol." Sky ambled back into the room, resumed his spot on the floor and refilled their drinks. Again. "It's simple to play. Basically, we take turns asking best-ever and worst-ever questions. Like say, it's my turn and you ask me to name the best movie ever. I'd say the 1992 classic *Army of Darkness*. Or, say it's your turn, and I choose for you best day ever. Then you'd tell the story of the day you met me. And don't give me that look. You know it was the best day of your life."

Carey knew better than to argue with Sky's

teasing when he knew what he'd said was the God's honest truth.

"Basically we take turns going from best-ever stories to worst-ever stories. See? Easy."

"You're a bit deranged, you know that, right?" Carey smiled despite any trepidation he felt over what this bit of entertainment might reveal.

"Part of my charm. I'll go first, which means I'll choose for you. And I choose best song ever."

"Easy. *Silly Love Songs*."

"Wait—what? Really?"

"Yes. Really. Shut up. It's a sweet song. And I like Paul McCartney. And it's my turn. I choose for you best TV show ever."

"*Buffy the Vampire Slayer*. Without question."

Carey would have rolled his eyes at such a dorky answer if he hadn't wholeheartedly agreed.

"Okay. Best date ever. Go."

"Oh, um. I thought this was just listing our favorite things, like movies and food and stuff."

"It is, but that's easy. And it gets boring fast. So go. Tell me about your best date ever."

Carey wasn't sure how to answer this one. Most of his dates rated on the sad side of the best-ever, worst-ever scale.

"Best date ever. Let's see. An invitation for a drink. Just casual. Then dinner. He cooks. And we chat all night. We talk about nothing, and we talk about everything. And we just … click. Then the kiss. A perfect kiss. And we make love and fall asleep knowing that there won't be any awkward, morning-after shit. None of those I-have-get-up-early-tomorrow excuses. No 'I can't see you in public, so can we keep this on the DL?' No worrying about whether he'll call. Because he does. None of the usual bullshit. Just perfect."

"Was that Stephen?"

"No. God, no. Not Stephen."

"So who was it? Who was the guy?"

"Well it hasn't actually happened. But that would be my best date ever. So…" He knew that, as far as best dates went, he wasn't exactly reaching for the stars.

"I'm pretty sure that's cheating."

"Why? You challenged me with best date ever. That's it. That's my best date ever. Just because it hasn't happened yet, doesn't mean it might not."

Sky watched Carey closely. Carey hoped he wasn't able to see the sadness that came with that confession. They were supposed to be dealing with Sky's heartache, after all, not adding Carey's to the mix.

"Okay, me. It's your turn to pick for me."

"Worst date ever."

"Easy. December nineteenth. The day my fiancée told me she didn't want to marry me."

Carey winced, wishing he could take it back. The last thing he wanted to do was put Sky on the spot and shine a light on the very reason they were here together in the first place.

"Oh shit, Sky. I'm sorry. I didn't mean—"

"You. Worst date ever." Sky barely skipped a beat.

"Um." Carey knew the answer to this. He didn't even have to think about it. But that didn't make it any easier to share. He no longer held feelings for the date in question, but that didn't make it any less humiliating. Beyond humiliating, actually. If it meant he could shine a light on something other than Sky's heartache, though, then he'd share. "His name was Shane." Carey sighed. "He took me to dinner at Sotto Sotto."

"Fancy."

"Right? I'd never been taken anywhere close to that nice before. So I figured he must have been really into me, right? He picked me up, dressed to the nines. Escorted me in on his arm. The maître d' showed us to our table. It was gorgeous. Shane ordered champagne and appetizers. I felt like a million bucks. I felt like I must have been something special to get this kind of treatment."

"When does the worst ever part happen, exactly?"

"Wait for it." Carey forced a chuckle. "So when Shane excused himself to use the washroom, I figured he had just gone to answer the call of nature, or just to wash his hands, freshen up. This place was *really* fancy. But then he was gone for, like, fifteen almost twenty minutes. So I went to check on him. You know, to see if he was OK. And he was … well, he was more than OK. Here I was all concerned that maybe something was wrong. Maybe he was ill. And there he was, up against the wall of this hoity-toity bathroom, dress pants around his ankles, while the maître d' was on his knees, showing him the extra-special VIP dishes of the evening."

"Holy shit. Holy shit, buddy—that really does suck. No pun intended."

"Nah. S'okay." Carey smiled. "It was a long time ago."

He thought carefully about his next challenge. He needed to lighten the mood. He just wasn't sure which direction to take things. In the end, he opted for simplicity.

"How about best pizza ever?"

"Lame."

"Why's it lame?" Carey realized his words were starting to slur and match the fuzziness in his head.

"Just is. Especially after what you just shared. But alright. Your choice. Best pizza ever. It was our senior year. We'd been out celebrating the very last of our exams but didn't want to completely tie one on because we had that road trip to NYC the next day, remember? And neither of us wanted to be praying to the porcelain god or in pain while trying to drive. So we picked up pizza from Amato and ate it in front of your laptop watching *Star Wars Episode IV*. Remember?"

Remember? Jesus. Of course, Carey remembered. How could he ever forget that night?

"Now you. Best kiss ever."

Fuck.

L.D. BLAKELEY

CHAPTER SIX

CAREY JUMPED to his feet, grabbed the now-empty pitcher, and headed back to the kitchen for a refill. He knew he couldn't share that. There was no way in hell he could tell Sky…

He didn't want to admit that his best kiss ever took place over a decade ago, in his tiny, shabby dorm room. Because as much as he cherished that moment, he knew how sad it was that his best kiss ever hadn't been real, had only been a fluke … and had been with a straight man. Hoping to bluff his way out of admitting the truth, Carey offered up a quick lie.

"Heath," he yelled back into the other room. "Remember Heath from third year?"

"Handsy Heath? The guy you said made you feel like he was trying to remove your adenoids with his tongue? Care to try again, this time with the truth?"

Carey stared at the floor and silently cursed his feeble poker face. He sure as hell didn't want to answer again and tell Sky the truth. He didn't want to admit that the best kiss he'd ever experienced had been something that had him wondering for weeks (months—who was he kidding?) afterward. Sky was straight, right? And it was almost a decade ago, so he likely didn't even remember. Right?

"WATCH IT! You're getting artichoke on the keyboard!"

Carey couldn't care less about the artichoke or the keyboard. What he did care about was the man pressed up next to him on his narrow dorm-room bed. Watching Star Wars *and eating pizza had been Sky's idea. Far be it for Carey to deny his best friend anything his heart desired.*

"Well, who eats pizza with artichokes, anyway?"

"At the moment, you are. And, considering you just inhaled four slices, I'd hazard a guess you don't exactly hate it."

"Maybe. Maybe I just like you and don't want to hurt your feelings." Sky grinned as he finished wiping off the laptop. Settling back against the headboard, in against Carey, he stretched his long legs out across the bed and leaned in closer, ostensibly for a better view of the movie. Carey's pulse sped up, and he could feel the heat being generated from Sky's proximity. He prayed his anatomy

wouldn't betray what he was thinking. He was sure Sky could hear his jackhammer heartbeat. But with Sky so close, practically breathing against his neck, he was helpless to stop his body's reaction. With a slight shimmy, he untucked his shirt and adjusted himself with as much stealth as he could manage with the object of his unrequited lust practically in his lap. The movement didn't go unnoticed, however, and he could feel the grin on Sky's face widen before he turned and saw the handsome smile for himself. He blushed crimson, hoping that the laptop wouldn't throw enough light for it to be noticeable.

"I should … um…"

Carey's words were silenced with the softest, sweetest, most heart-wrenching touch he could have ever imagined. A caress, barely a brush of lips, Sky's kiss was apprehensive, almost reverent. His left hand hovered, nervously, above Carey's collarbone and eventually came to rest, with fingers splayed delicately near his throat.

His brain reeled and tried to form cohesive thought, but the only thing that registered were the crackles of electricity currently sparking from his head to his toes. Warm breath mingled, and Carey could feel the tentative dart of Sky's tongue against the seam of his lips. Carey opened to him, allowing him entrance and savoring the heady taste of Sky's mouth.

Sky. Oh my god, Sky.

Sky is kissing me.

Reaching out cautiously, he slowly tangled his fingers into the soft, silky hair that curled in at Sky's nape and let himself melt into the moment. Carey continued to taste him, letting his tongue run across his pouty bottom lip, only to return to its tangle with Sky's own. And Sky didn't stop him. He didn't stop him, so Carey continued. And as he urged Sky to feel a fraction of what he was feeling, a moan slipped from his lips. It was so completely unexpected that he had to pull away and look at him. There was something in Sky's eyes that he couldn't quite read. Fear? Anger? Desire? But before he could interpret the expression, the moment was over. Sky was off the bed and out the door before he knew what was happening.

SKY STUMBLED into the kitchen behind him, dragging Carey from his lust-filled memories.

"Y'can't just fuck off and avoid the question. Hafta play by the rules. C'mon. Best kiss ever. Go."

Carey stood stock-still, unable to speak or move.

"How 'bout I go first, then." Sky taunted. "*My* best kiss ever. You were there. Don't you remember?"

What?

"Time to cut you off, mister. You've had enough." Carey nervously cleared his throat, hoping he sounded nonchalant.

"Wasn't drunk *that* night, Carey. I was scared. But I knew what I was doing. Well, not exactly *knew.* I was so fucking scared. But I figured you never would. And I wanted to kiss you." Sky stepped closer to Carey, backing him up until his ass hit the edge of the counter. Bracing his hands on either side of Carey's hips, he moved in until their faces were a mere breath apart. "Wanted to kiss you more than anything," he said, ghosting his lips across Carey's.

"Sky," Carey hesitated. "What're you doing?" There was a brief catch in his voice as he tried to steady his breathing.

"Kissing you, dumbass. You always were a bit slow on the uptake. You were like that in school, and you are still." Sky closed the distance between them and pressed his firm, full lips against Carey's. He moved one hand up under Carey's shirt, tracing a pattern around his navel, as the other gripped the unsteady man's hip. Carey could feel his cock, already solid, nestled firmly against Sky's thigh. Somewhere, in the back of his brain, a voice was screaming at him to stop. But the onslaught of Sky's mouth rendered him helpless.

Sky slowly rocked his hips as he changed his tack and lazily licked his way into the hollow of Carey's collarbone. A sweetly torturous heat radiated to his every nerve ending, and an unfamiliar tightness took hold in Carey's chest.

"Mmm … you taste good, Carey."

Sky's voice had an intoxicating effect on Carey's senses at the best of times, but the contact his mouth and hands made against his sensitive flesh had his head swimming. Common sense told Carey he should call a halt to this now while there was still a chance he could save face once they both sobered up.

"I'm sorry, Sky. I shouldn't…" Oh, but he wanted to.

"No. Carey." Sky reached out and wrapped a handful of Carey's hair around his fingertips and brought their faces back together.

"Are you sure?" Carey breathed against Sky's lips.

"Mmm-hmm." He captured Carey's mouth again and sucked the air from his already constricted lungs.

Carey traced Sky's lips with a needy tongue, and he opened to him with a beautiful moan. Sky darted his tongue against Carey's, sending a lightning-quick jolt through him. Carey's entire body was on fire, and from nothing more than a kiss.

Sky still pressed his hips against Carey's, and Carey's head spun as he ran his tongue across Sky's teeth and mapped his hot, sweet mouth. Sky kissed him back with a sudden and fierce passion, violently wrapping his tongue around Carey's and plunging into the depths of his mouth. Carey could feel that he was no longer the only one sporting rather obvious proof of his arousal. Sky's hard length rubbed against Carey as he hooked an impossibly long leg around the back of Carey's calf and began to grind.

"Ohhh," Carey moaned unabashedly.

"Carey…" Sky whimpered, and Carey was certain he'd never heard anything sound so sexy in his entire life.

Carey latched onto Sky's neck with a hungry mouth and grazed a peaked nipple with eager fingertips. He inched one hand up under Sky's shirt and nibbled on the tender flesh—knowing that he would more than likely leave a mark. But Carey didn't care. He couldn't. If this was his one-night reprieve from a lifetime of yearning, then he had to take whatever Sky was willing to give.

Fuck me. I'm totally going to worst-friend-ever hell.

Carey slowly tugged Sky's shirt up and over his chest, carefully watching for any sign that he'd gone too far. But Sky was happy to comply. In fact, he was quick to raise his arms over his head and allow the shirt to be removed completely. His beauty was breathtaking. Seeing Sky's naked flesh in passing was one thing. Having it under his fingertips was something else entirely. Carey trailed his fingers across Sky's chest and ran the tips down to just above his abdomen—not sure if he should push by going further.

Sky watched Carey's every move with quiet fascination. And when Carey allowed himself to meet Sky's eyes, he was met with a gaze that made him shudder and his blood boil hot. Lust. He saw lust staring back at him from those beautiful green eyes.

Carey hungrily pounced and crushed his mouth to Sky's with such force he was afraid he'd draw blood. But if any of the same fears were running through Sky's head, he did a fine job of disguising them. A deep, predatory growl escaped him as he thrust Carey back against the counter, shoved his hands into Carey's waistband, ripped open his fly, and exposed Carey's heated flesh to the chill of the room.

"Fuck, Sky!" Carey hissed.

"Show me what to do, Care." His eyes were pleading and full of lust. "Show me what you want. What you need."

Carey pressed his mouth against Sky's throat, tasting him, marking him. *Oh, god.*

"Just let me touch you, Sky. Taste you." *Love you…*

Carey felt Sky's hand snake down across his abdomen and cautiously wrap around his painfully hard cock. He twitched in Sky's grasp, feeling the world spin out of control.

"Oh God." Carey's voice hitched.

"Is that okay?" Sky asked as he began slowly pumping his fist in a taunting rhythm.

"Ah, Jesus! Sky," he panted. "So much yes!"

He felt Sky drag his thumb across the swollen, sensitive tip, and Carey could feel himself leak across Sky's nimble fingers.

"Mmm…" Anything more than moaning was beyond him.

Carey grabbed Sky by the hair, switched their positions, and backed the taller man up against the counter. Dropping to his knees, he pinned Sky's hips in place and quickly worked his jeans to the floor.

Christ, almighty. Commando.

"So fucking beautiful." Carey allowed himself the luxury of drinking in Sky's exquisite form, knowing this could be his one chance to gorge on what he'd always wanted.

Sky's cock was thick, hard, and arched proudly against his taut stomach. The head glistened with precum, and Carey lapped greedily like he was feeding on ambrosia.

"Oh. Fuck, yeah," Sky whimpered as Carey suckled.

Wrapping his hand around the base of Sky's cock, Carey buried his nose in dark curls. He smelled like sweat, soap, and arousal—so distinctly male, so distinctly Sky.

Carey rolled Sky's heavy balls in the palm of

his hand as he ran his tongue from the base of that magnificent cock to the delicious, spongy tip. He listened, blissfully, to the kitten-like moans his touch was eliciting. Sky's hips jerked as Carey slowly took the head of Sky's cock into his mouth and looked up to make sure that his friend was still fine with the proceedings.

"Please, Carey," he whispered.

With that consent, Carey swallowed Sky entirely. His cock was hard and throbbing against the back of his throat, and Carey wanted to stay right there forever. Sky's panting and moaning was all the encouragement Carey needed to begin furiously bobbing his head up and down, adopting a heated rhythm as he sucked Sky into his mouth.

He felt Sky's balls tighten. And from the vicious cursing and babbling filling the room, he knew he wouldn't last much longer.

"C'mon, Sky." Carey lifted his mouth momentarily. "Come for me, babe."

Carey resumed his efforts with a hum, knowing that the vibrations in his throat would be all it would take to send Sky over the edge.

Sky's hips snapped as he shouted his imminent release. "Oh yes … fuck! Oh, God—Carey! Aaaaah!" Carey felt Sky explode in his mouth, and he eagerly swallowed every hot, precious drop—savoring and memorizing Sky's unique and delicious tang.

"Mmm. Holy shit, Care…" Sky's chest heaved, his breathing labored.

Carey stood to his full height and wrapped his arms around Sky's waist, searching for any sign of fear or uneasiness. There was none. Only complete contentment and, dare he think it, bliss?

"Sky?"

"Hmm?"

"You okay?"

"Well, let's see. My best friend just gave me *the* most incredible blowjob, so I'd have to say the answer to that question is yes. Final answer— yes." He grinned.

"Really?"

"Really."

"No weirdness?"

"Nope."

Sky captured Carey's mouth again, not bothered in the slightest that he could obviously taste himself on the other man's lips. Unfortunately for Carey, his cock was still achingly hard and Sky was doing a fine job of making it harder still. Carey, unconsciously, began to slowly and steadily rock his hips against Sky.

"Your turn," Sky murmured against Carey's neck, trailing kisses across his throat. He grasped Carey's rigid cock, tracing the tip, again, with his thumb and letting Carey frantically fuck his fist.

"Sky…. Oh, God. Sky!"

"You like that?" he whispered between kisses. Carey was close. So close. His heart was racing, and he could feel his orgasm beginning to build in his toes. "Love you, Carey." It was barely audible.

*Jesusfuck*what?

Carey wasn't sure if Sky had said the words or if they were part of his elaborate and absurd imagination. Either way, it was all the trigger he needed. He grasped roughly at Sky's shoulders and came into his tightly gripped hand.

"Sky—fuuuck!"

White-hot pinpricks exploded against Carey's eyelids, and liquid heat coursed through his veins. He reached for Sky's face and drove his tongue deep into his mouth, needing to taste the other man as he rode this wave of ecstasy. Sky met his tongue with an equaled passion, leaving Carey completely blissed out on sensation.

When his breathing returned to normal, Carey realized that Sky was cradling his face and gently stroking his hair. He also realized that he was trembling uncontrollably. Unable to still the heaving shivers racking his frame, Carey turned his face toward Sky's chest, wrapped his arms tightly around his waist, and allowed himself to be held.

With sure, strong hands stroking gently across Carey's shoulders, Sky held him still.

"C'mon. Let's go to bed, Carey."

And with no thought as to what daybreak would bring, Carey let his best friend in the world lead him by the hand and take him to bed.

CHAPTER SEVEN

CAREY AWOKE once during the night, wondering just how many drinks he'd had and if he'd, in fact, dreamt the entire thing. Had he imagined the soft curve of Sky's ass and the unbelievable taste of his rigid cock? Was the way Sky's eyes rolled back as he came something Carey had simply imagined? Was fucking his way to a soul-scorching orgasm in Sky's tight, rugged fist merely something he'd constructed in his vivid and filthy fantasies?

The wall of heat plastered against his back, though, dispelled any notion that the previous night's events hadn't happened. A muscled arm rested lazily over his hip, and he could feel hot puffs of breath against his neck. Wriggling slightly against the man all but wrapped around him, he realized that the muscled abs and pecs weren't the only hard thing pressed tight against him.

"Mmmm, nice." In a sleep-induced haze, Sky pulled Carey closer and began deliberately rocking his hips against the crease of Carey's naked ass. Carey could feel the delicious ache start to build as he matched Sky's gentle movement thrust for thrust. A swell of heat pooled in his groin, and Carey could feel Sky's hips take on a more purposeful pace.

Before his brain had a chance to convince him that taking this thing with Sky—whatever *this* was—any further could easily destroy over a decade of friendship, he turned in his lover's arms and swiftly flipped Sky onto his back. With painstaking attention, he paid tribute to Sky with his lips, tongue, and fingertips. Carey rained small, delicate kisses over the taller man's eyelids while with his fingers he sought purchase in Sky's sleep-disheveled hair. Carey took his time to taste every inch of his delectable friend, moving ever slowly down to lick swaths across his throat. With his tongue, he sought out and traced the shell of Sky's ear before taking his mouth in a searing kiss. Sky opened to him instantly, and their tongues danced a wicked, dirty tango.

"Jesus, Sky," Carey gasped, staring in disbelief and with awe at the lust-heady eyes gazing back at him, when he finally came up for air. *If there's a sight more fucking sublime than that, then I'd like someone to show me.* Strong fingers grasped at the back of his head, pulling him back to Sky's perfect kiss-swollen mouth.

Carey could feel the room close in on them as the delicious sounds of their mouths and tongues tangling combined exquisitely with the music of skin on skin, moans and sighs. The delightfully obscene symphony had Carey hard as a rock and secure in the knowledge that this was *not* going to last long.

"Sky," he panted and tried to slow his movements. Eagerly seeking the friction he clearly craved desperately, Sky continued to grind up into Carey's sensitive flesh. "Sky! Sky—stop. Just … one minute." Carey pinned the other man's hips in an attempt at gaining some semblance of control.

"Carey. Why do you hate me?" The wicked, teasing grin belied the breathy voice and stern expression on Sky's face.

"Mmm. Definitely don't hate you. Most definitely don't hate this." Carey steadied his breathing before asking, "What are we doing, Sky?"

"Fucking."

"We're fucking?"

"Aren't we?"

"Do you have condoms?" Even though he

knew the answer, a part of Carey hoped otherwise.

"Um. No, but…"

"Then we're not fucking."

"Carey. You're killing me. You know what I mean."

"Do I?"

"Care, we're naked and sweaty with dicks hard enough to pound six-inch spikes through a board. You're on top of me, and my legs are spread like a drunk cheerleader at prom."

Leave it to Sky to bring an '80s Val Kilmer movie reference into the bedroom.

"You really aren't freaked out right now, are you?" It was more a revelation than a question. "I mean Jesus, Sky. You're straight."

"I think bendy is a better description, don't you?"

"Since when, though?" Despite the absence of blood to his brain, Carey was still having a tough time parsing this Sky with the one he'd always known.

"Since always. You just never noticed."

"Fuck me." It came out like one word, barely audible.

"Well you already put the kibosh on that. But seriously," Sky glanced down at Carey's naked and willing body and gestured to his own, "If somebody doesn't come soon, I am going to throw your ass out into a snowbank!"

"That sounds unpleasant. This, however, is *very* pleasant." Carey quickly shimmied down the length of Sky's body and swallowed him to the root in one fell swoop.

"Ngggah! Carey!"

Carey looked up to see Sky tossing his head frantically from side to side. His slack jaw and heavy-lidded eyes were something Carey could definitely get used to seeing.

Hollowing his cheeks to create an oh-so-indecent vacuum, Carey slowly began to suck Sky in and out of his mouth and set about making him fly apart at the seams.

"Wait!" Sky was gasping through his words. "Wait. Carey. Wanna taste you, too. Can we … at the same time? Please?"

Good. Christ.

"Jesus, Sky." It was barely a whisper. "Are you sure?"

"Damn sure."

Carey deftly flipped his position so his hips were in line with Sky's shoulders, rolled to his side, and pulled gently at his lover so that they faced each other. The musky scent of arousal, sweat, and Sky was almost more than Carey could stand. His mouth went dry, and he held his breath, knowing that his swollen cock was so close to the most beautiful mouth he'd ever seen.

The first tentative flickers of Sky's tongue were almost his undoing; he continued to hold his breath and somehow managed to stroke Sky with his hand.

"Oh, *fuck*!" Carey felt the entirety of Sky's hot, wet mouth wrap around the spongy head of his cock. Those delicate licks were now far more assured as they worried his sensitive ridge and flickered across the tip. Sky was a quick learner. Then again, maybe this wasn't so new to him, after all. Carey ignored that idea and every ugly emotion that came with it. He closed his eyes and let himself drift, enjoying every electric sensation that shattered his nerve endings. And when Sky stroked one strong, delicate finger across Carey's balls and down toward his asshole, Carey's brain crackled and shorted out. *Too much! Too much!* He cried out his release in one great, shuddering spasm.

Carey shivered, convulsed, and almost forgot what he was doing. Almost. Until he felt the big body against him tighten like a spring, then break loose with a mighty snap. "Ahhh, fuck! Carey!" And as Sky came, jetting hot strands of semen all over Carey's chest, shoulder, and chin, he remembered exactly what they were doing. He also did his damnedest to ignore that niggling voice in the back of head screaming at him that he was going to walk away from this with a shattered heart and short a best friend. He couldn't bring himself to care that Sky was relatively new to this. Or was he? Either way, Carey knew he should be the one to know better. Instead, he let his tongue snake out to lick his own chin clean before leaning forward to apply the exact same treatment to the tip of Sky's obscenely wet and quivering cock.

WHEN CAREY woke the next day, it was to an empty bed. The spot where Sky had lain was now cold, and Carey wondered for a moment if he'd slept there at all. But, when he rolled over and hugged the pillow up to his face, he could still smell traces of Sky's shampoo, soap, and sweat. And the unmistakable smell of sex permeated the room.

The sound of his friend's raised voice coming from the living room shook him fully awake, and he rolled out of bed in search of a clean pair of boxer briefs.

Padding barefoot down the hallway, sporting a smile of the sated, Carey realized Sky was on the phone; he halted as he heard the strained half of Sky's conversation.

"I know … Yes, I'm sure … No, I really don't want that either … OK … I will … Yes, shortly … Bye."

When he was sure Sky had ended the call,

Carey crept up behind him and wrapped his arms around the taller man before gently kissing the back of his bare shoulder. "Morning, gorgeous."

"Morning." Sky hugged Carey's arms against his chest with a soft caress.

"That didn't sound like a very Happy New Year kinda conversation. Work?" Carey knew that Sky's job held a lot of responsibility and could oftentimes result in panicked phone calls, even on statutory holidays.

But when Sky didn't answer right away, Carey knew. He felt the slight shift in the other man's stance and heard the troubled sigh that escaped in place of a response. He knew before he asked. He had to have known. But he pressed on, needing to hear it, needing to know that he'd been right all along: that crossing that line was a step too far.

"Sky?"

"It was Elise." Sky's voice was barely audible.

Carey turned and pushed free of the embrace.

"She needs me. Her dad…" Sky furrowed his brow and waved his phone as though that explained things. "I need to go back to the city. I'm sorry."

The way Sky stared at the floor said it all. Carey knew. He had known last night, but he had chosen to traipse blindly forward, allowing years of longing to throw caution to the wind. He knew, and now he was fucked.

"Right. Of course. I'll just, um…"

Carey bolted from the room. Then he dressed and threw belongings into his suitcase at breakneck speed. He didn't give a shit if anything got left behind. He just had to get out, get out and get far away from the crushing weight of the eye contact Sky refused to make.

The drive back to the city was agonizingly long. In reality, the trip took just under three hours. But it seemed like an eternity, an eternity for Carey to replay every detail of the past few days in his head. He'd finally gotten the one thing he never dared ask for. But what was the old adage? Don't fuck with a fantasy. And now he knew the truth of that all too well.

Worst New Year ever.

L.D. BLAKELEY

CHAPTER EIGHT

"MR. ENGLISH? Mr. English, did you want me to finish with these order forms?"

Carey had been sitting at his desk for the better part of an hour, staring blankly into his computer monitor, hypnotized by the angry ping of his instant messenger. He hadn't heard Kelly, the newest member of the Carey's Catering & Events family, timidly trying to get his attention. He hadn't even realized she was standing on the other side of his desk until Andrew had walked up beside her and snapped his fingers so close to Carey's face he could almost feel them graze his chin.

Andrew ushered the girl out with a reassuring smile, closed the door quietly, and walked across the office to delicately perch on the edge of

Carey's desk.

"What?" Carey blinked up at Andrew's friendly, unfaltering smile.

"Are you kidding me? You've been a space cadet for the past week, Care Bear. That poor girl was trying to get your attention for a good ten minutes. You've ignored phone calls. No—don't try to deny it. I've heard you let them ring through to voice mail. Which isn't like you at all. I'm guessing you haven't slept or eaten anything in days. And I'm going to go out on a limb and say that all of this has something to do with that tall drink of a best friend of yours and how you rang in the New Year."

Carey gazed blankly at his keyboard, afraid to make eye contact with Andrew, afraid that if he allowed that unspoken communication to happen, the truth would be out there and he'd shatter to dust and blow away.

"I can sit here all day, handsome. Up to you whether or not it's in silence. But I will say this— whatever it is, it can't be that bad. It can't be worth whatever torture you're dreaming up in that scary, scattered head. It can't—"

"I slept with Sky!" Carey blurted out before he was aware that his mouth and brain were once again united. He looked up at Andrew, eyes wild, bleary, and lost.

"*Daamn*!"

"I know."

"But—" Andrew pursed his lips and stared quizzically. "—he's straight."

"That's what I thought, too."

"So…"

"So, I don't know. I don't know anything."

"Help me out here, Care Bear. You've been in love with this guy for years—shut up, I know you have so don't bother arguing with me. You finally get him into bed and now, what, you're worried it'll affect global warming? I mean—I'm really not seeing the problem."

Carey snorted and shook his head.

"Oh, almost a smile! Fantastic! So tell me—" Andrew leaned forward and lowered his voice. "—was it *bad*? That'd certainly explain the long face."

If only. Carey wished it had been bad. At least then he could tell himself that everything he'd felt had only been wishful thinking. He wouldn't have to tell himself that he'd seen something of those feelings mirrored in his best friend.

But it was so far removed from bad that he was willing to bet he'd spend the rest of his life trying to achieve even a fraction of what he'd felt that night. But Sky was straight. And now he had Elise back. He could return to his *straight* world, get *straight* married, and live happily *straight* ever after.

"I don't want to talk about it, Drew. Please? Can we not talk about it right now?"

Despite several frantic texts from Sky explaining that Elise's father had been rushed into emergency surgery and—broken engagement or not—she'd asked Sky to come be by her side, the big cement fortress around Carey's heart was slowly being rebuilt brick by unhappy brick. If Sky could run off that quickly at her beck and call, how long would it be before they were back in each other's arms and setting a new date for their nuptials?

"Fine." Drew sighed. "But I'm taking you to Boutique for martinis."

"I really don't feel up to cocktails right now, Drew."

"Don't be ridiculous. I'm taking you out, buying you at least three martinis—one of which I plan to spike with half an Ambien—and then I'm taking you home so you can get some sleep. Those bags under your eyes are *not* designer, honey. You need to take better care of yourself."

Several cocktails—hold the Ambien—later and Carey was ready to acknowledge Drew was right. He had needed to unwind. And the alcohol did a lovely job of glazing over his ragged emotions, at least temporarily.

He still wasn't ready to face Sky, however, even though the messages from him were starting to pile up. He knew ignoring them was taking the coward's way out, but he preferred to think of it as self-preservation. He could play the avoidance game a little while longer, but Sky wasn't about to disappear. Ten-plus years of friendship didn't just fade into the ether and Carey knew he'd have to face him eventually. He just wasn't ready to live in a world where he'd finally had a taste of what he'd always craved, only to have to walk away. The reality of it twisted and wrenched in his guts because he knew that's exactly what he was going to have to live with. For now, though, he could wallow.

"You looked like you could use another one of these." Drew plunked down another dirty martini and clinked his own against the edge of the glass.

"This needs to be the last one, though." He sipped the drink in question, knowing he'd be in hellish shape tomorrow morning if he kept knocking them back at this rate.

"I'll tuck you in myself if need be." Drew perched on his barstool and scanned the crowd. "Besides, I don't plan to stay much longer anyway. Just long enough to drink a smile onto your face. If I don't get a full eight hours all this pretty starts to tarnish. And nobody wants that."

Carey shook his head, rolling his eyes in disbelief, as he took in his co-worker's flawless appearance. Beauty, aided by sleep or otherwise, was hardly something he lacked.

"Hold that thought." Carey raised his glass, taking one more sip. "Nature calls," he added, nodding toward the washrooms. "Be right back."

"You better be," Drew answered. "Don't you dare think about ducking out of here before I've properly plied you with alcohol."

"Wouldn't dream of it," he called over his shoulder as he headed through the crowd. Bodies were pressed against each other everywhere he looked, some locked in serious clinches while others simply swayed to the music. Several men even gave Carey the eye. A few of them would have piqued his interest a few weeks ago. But none of them were Sky. Which sucked. Because what better way to get over someone than to get under someone new. Wasn't that what Drew always told him?

Speaking of which … he'd only been gone ten minutes but by the time Carey returned to their table Drew was flirting up a storm with a handsome stranger. At least, he assumed the man was handsome. With his back to Carey, it was hard to tell, but what he could see was nice.

I'll just make myself scarce.

Downing the remains of his drink and reaching for his coat, Carey shot a knowing wink at Drew. As he bundled up and caught a glimpse of the man's face, Carey was floored.

"Stephen?" His voice cracked with surprise rather than emotion. There was a time he'd have been beyond thrilled to see the man here. But that was then. Now he was simply confused.

"Carey. Hi."

"Wait," Drew interrupted. "You're Carey's Stephen?" He let out a disgusted sigh. "God, why do all the pretty ones come with so much drama?"

"You do know this is a gay bar, right?" It was a dig, but Carey couldn't help himself.

"I do."

"So…" Carey raised an eyebrow, waiting for a response.

"I guess I deserve that." Stephen tucked a lock of hair behind one ear and bowed his head momentarily before continuing. "I owe you a huge apology, Carey. I know that."

"So what, you're out now? But you couldn't be bothered with me?" He glanced at Drew who gave him a thumbs up.

"I hope you don't really believe that." Stephen's voice was small as he jammed his hands in his front pockets.

"Why on earth would I think otherwise?"

Stephen frowned. "If I could do it all over again, Carey, I would. I'd be out and proud and by your side. But I know I fucked up."

Carey was taken aback. He had no idea what to

say. Once upon a time he'd have paid good money to hear Stephen speak those words. Now?

He was at a loss. "I don't know what to do with any of this," he finally admitted.

"Nothing." Stephen shrugged. "I know I don't deserve your forgiveness but I'm sorry, Carey. I couldn't be honest with myself or anyone else in my world when we were together, and I let a good thing get away."

"Oh." Carey was struck with the sudden realization that he was finally hearing what he'd always wanted from Stephen and he didn't care.

"You'll always be my biggest regret."

Shit.

A light bulb went off. Suddenly aware of his own potential impending regret, Carey knew it was time to man up and face Sky. It was time to get over himself and put it all out there, or he'd be back in a bar just like this and in the same boat as Stephen.

"I have to go." He glanced at Drew who waved him off with a wink and salute of his glass.

"You do you, baby. I'll see you at work."

"Bye Stephen. I just … thank you." He flashed a genuine smile and drew the zipper on his coat up tight.

One way or another, things were going to be hashed out with Sky. Either their friendship would survive or it wouldn't. But at least he'd know where he stood.

No regrets.

L.D. BLAKELEY

CHAPTER NINE

DESPITE THE martinis, Carey felt oddly lucid. Adrenaline worked wonders when it needed to. As he struggled with his key in the lock, the door swung wide to reveal the very object of his self-inflicted torture.

"Sky? What the hell?"

"Whisky sour?" Sky held out a highball with a rueful smile.

Epiphany or not, Carey had hoped for at least the night to mull things over. He might be ready to lay his cards on the table, but he needed a minute before he'd be ready to hear Sky's reaction. He took the glass and knocked back half its contents in one swallow. "How did you get in here?"

"Used my key."

"*Your* key? What—"

"Well, your key, really. The one you gave me four years ago when I crashed on your couch. After Julie kicked me out. Remember?" Ah, yes. Julie—one of many in a long line of Sky's exes.

"That still doesn't tell me what the hell you're doing here, Sky." Exasperation and alcohol had shortened Carey's fuse.

"Fixing you a drink. Making you dinner."

"What the … Why?"

"So you can have your best date ever." He shrugged.

"So you just thought you'd—wait, you cooked?"

"Of course not. You and I both know I can't cook for shit. Pancakes from a mix don't count. And YouTube can only teach a guy like me so much. I got takeout, though. I'm a pretty good heater upper. And I can set a mean table." Sky was grinning widely and bouncing on the balls of his feet.

"Sky—" Carey sighed loudly, giving himself a mental shake "—seriously. I'm not in the mood for this. Go home."

"Pretty hard for this to be a date, if I leave you here alone."

"Sky, this isn't funny. You've had your little adventure in Boys Town." When Sky started to interrupt, Carey cut him off and continued, "And, yeah, I was there—it *was* incredible. But I'll be damned if I'll plan your wedding *and* be your dirty little secret." He knew he delivered that more harshly than he'd planned. But fuck it. He was through walking on eggshells. "Go home. I'm sure Elise is wondering where the hell you are."

"First of all, there's still no wedding, Carey. Secondly, Elise has nothing to do with this … with us." Sky's tone was suddenly somber. "You'd know that if you'd bothered to reply to any one of the hundred or so messages I've left you in the past week."

Carey stood silently, afraid of lashing out further.

"Carey. You left so quickly I didn't know what to do. I wanted to explain to you…"

"Explain what? That you made a mistake? That you were going back to Elise? That she called, and you came running? I was there, Sky. I'm already aware of what happened."

"*No!*" Before he could step further into his foyer, Carey was unceremoniously pinned by the shoulders against the far wall, with two hundred pounds of Skyler Wood staring him in the face. "No! You're not aware, Carey! You're not aware of what happened at all. You have no idea what happened because you've been MIA for an entire fucking week, Carey! If you'd bothered to pick up the phone or answered even one of my messages, then you might. You might have some clue. But you don't. You have no idea how much I … how much…" And as quickly as the anger had erupted, it was gone. "How fucking much I miss you. How fucking much I need you."

Not trusting his mouth to reply while his brain wasn't entirely certain what was happening, Carey said nothing. He watched Sky's face, looking for something that would help him make sense of the words he'd just heard. What he saw was a quiet desperation. He saw a face silently pleading with him to understand without any further prodding.

But Carey waited. He waited for Sky to continue because he was struck mute with the fear that his far-too-vivid imagination was once again inventing things that weren't there. Things like the improbable notion that Sky might feel one iota of what Carey felt.

"Sky, can you … can you please let go of me?" he asked when he realized Sky wasn't going to continue. "I don't … I really don't know … Fuck." Why couldn't he articulate one single thought? "Just…"

When he was free to move, Carey crossed his arms over his chest, with his half-empty drink dangling precariously in one hand, in a move he guessed looked more confrontational that he intended. Truth be told, the move was more out of self-preservation than anything else. Physical contact with Sky seemed to short out his brain, and if there was ever a conversation he wanted to be well and truly alert for, this was the one.

"Just listen to me, Carey." Sky gently took the tumbler from Cary, offering up his other hand at the same time. "Please?" Without a thought, Carey allowed Sky to take him by the hand and lead him into the living room. He sat at one end of the sofa, waiting for Sky to continue. But, instead of sitting next to him, Sky knelt on the floor, placing both hands on Carey's thighs as he looked up through dark lashes, pleadingly.

"Ever wonder why I can't keep a girlfriend, Carey?

"I have. I've been wondering for a long time now. No matter how many times I try, I get dumped. And I bent over backward for every single one of those women, Care. Every single one. I never cheated. I always remembered birthdays. Anniversaries. All of it. But none of it was ever enough. And I really could never figure it out. Until now. Until New Year's Eve. Until we…" Sky cleared his throat and continued.

"Elise knew. I didn't even know, but she did. She said she kept hoping that eventually, if she loved me enough, then I'd be able to feel the same way. But I couldn't. I tried. But she wasn't you, Carey."

"Sky, you don't—"

"Yes, Carey. I do. And, maybe it took a few too many drinks and a stupid junior high school game to make me realize. Or make you realize. Or make me realize you realized. Fuck. Whatever. The point is. I do. Realize, that is."

"What is it that you think you realize, Sky?"

"Jesus fucking Christ, Carey! Not even you're that obtuse," growled Sky as he claimed Carey's lips in a kiss that Carey feared would surely stop his heart. It was crushing, a kiss meant to possess and to claim. It was long and hot and so sweet. And, when Carey felt Sky's tongue sweep against his own, he knew that any lingering doubts that he might still have weren't going to get a chance to speak up anytime soon.

A shiver crept through Carey, and a primal moan erupted from deep within his chest as Sky trailed a searing path of kisses and licks toward the top button of his shirt. With clever fingers, he deftly untucked and unbuttoned while Carey realized he was being too passive a participant in this erotic dance. Reaching out to card his fingers through Sky's hair, Carey felt an answering shiver run through Sky and delighted in the accompanying sigh that escaped the other man's lips.

Making quick work of Carey's shirt, Sky used one hand to unbuckle the belt at Carey's waist while the other unzipped his pants. Carey was lost in sensation and could only whimper and lift his hips as Sky tugged his pants and boxers off in one quick move. He watched, through hooded lids, as Sky ducked his head and began to nibble and lick at Carey's thighs. Sky grazed his teeth along the sensitive flesh and, as Carey wantonly allowed his legs to spread further apart, Sky sank in his teeth and he moaned aloud.

"Sky. Ahhh…" Carey writhed as Sky sucked greedily—no doubt marking Carey's tender, pale skin. With that carnal realization, Carey groaned savagely as his hips began to thrust of their own accord.

Sky stilled Carey's movements and gently lifted Carey's knees, placing his feet on the edge of the sofa. Carey watched Sky lower his face and nuzzle at his groin. He trembled as Sky began to kiss and taste and let his tongue slowly map the entire length of his engorged cock. When Sky took the head into his mouth to gently suck away the glistening drops of precum that had begun to form, Carey was thankful to already be splayed on the sofa and not standing. There was no way his knees wouldn't have buckled. The steady rhythm Sky kept up with his fist and the wicked teasing of his tongue had Carey quickly teetering on the edge.

Carey's fingers gripped Sky's hair tightly as he shook and cried out.

"Feels good, yeah?" Sky's breath caressed Carey's overheated balls. "This'll feel even better," he promised as with his tongue he bathed Carey's tightened sac and darted further back to slowly taste the entrance to his lover's trembling body.

Sky's tongue worked a teasing pattern of licking and thrusting, driving Carey into a gasping frenzy. "Sky," he panted. "Sky, stop. You have to—"

Before Carey could utter another word, the hot, pointed tip of Sky's tongue breached his hole. The dual sensations of his best friend tongue-fucking him and jerking his cock at the same time sent Carey over the edge with an undignified scream. He flopped back on the sofa like a rag doll, trying to still his breathing and clinging to Sky like a lifeline. When his heart slowed somewhat and he could breathe without a constant rasp, he reached for Sky, only to have his hand lazily batted away.

"S'okay, Carey. M'good."

"Holy fuck, Sky, you sure as hell don't give head like you were straight two weeks ago," Carey panted. "Have you been Googling with the safe search off?"

"Ha-ha. Very cute," Sky deadpanned, as he adjusted himself with a slight grimace. "I hope you have clean laundry because I totally need a pair of your boxers."

"Oh, shit! Did you…?"

"I did. So clearly, I can't leave anytime soon."

"Then I guess I'll have to keep you."

"Yep." Sky crawled up next to Carey, draped himself, inelegantly, on top of him and stared.

"So you fixed dinner?" Carey asked, knowing full well the answer.

"Yup. And drinks." Sky grinned, and Carey couldn't help but mirror it back.

"And … the talking?"

"For *ages*." Sky feigned exasperation.

"So—" Carey nipped at Sky's bottom lip, taking it into his own and gently sucking. "—making love…"

"Fuck, yes. Definitely more of that."

"And tomorrow?"

"Look, I know day-after phone calls were part of your best-date-ever request list, but I really planned to keep you in bed all weekend. Will it be a deal breaker if I don't get up just to call you—what with you already being right next to me, naked and all?

"Hmm. Maybe not." Carey laughed against Sky's lips.

"Best date ever."

"Yes, Mr. Darcy. It certainly is."

THE END

ABOUT THE AUTHOR

A pragmatist with a romantic soul & a dirty mind, L.D. is a fan of horror movies, hot sex, and Happily Ever Afters. Easily distracted by shiny things, she's a slightly neurotic, highly ambitious dreamer who enjoys dabbling in photography & pretending she can carry a tune.

In another life, L.D. was a newspaper reporter, an entertainment & music writer, travel writer, website content editor, and a marketing shill. Now she prefers to spend her time writing hot, steamy fiction with a healthy dose of romance.

Although she dreams of living some place isolated with an endless supply of wine and an infinite number of titles on her eReader, she currently lives in downtown Toronto with her husband and their rock star cat.

Visit L.D. online at www.ldblakeley.com

ALSO BY L.D. BLAKELEY

The Power of Peppermint

The most wonderful time of the year?

When Jamison Pritchett is roped into replacing the mall photographer at Santa's Village a week before Christmas, he's certain he'll be spending the holidays recovering from a nervous breakdown. A throng of sugar-frenzied kids might be enough to send this uptight photographer back into the darkroom permanently. Inappropriate thoughts about his far-too-attractive—and far-too-young—assistant aren't helping fight that urge to hide, either.

For Noah Hawkins, adulting is a snap. Too bad relationships aren't. With his business temporarily closed for repairs, he's happy to help his sister out of a jam, even if the costume he's given to wear borders on obscene. Constantly being mistaken for a teenager is no treat either, especially when he discovers his temporary new co-worker is sexy as hell and 15 years his senior.

Can Noah convince Jamison that age is just a number? Or will Jamison resist the gift Santa seems to be handing him on a platter?

From Evernight Publishing:

Parker's Profile

Parker Knowles needs a date. No, really. If he can't find one by Valentine's Day, he's agreed to let his sister fix him up. And quite frankly, he'd rather chew off his own arm than go out with someone of his sister's choosing.

Internet phenom, Lane Steadman, has offered to show Parker the art of the perfect selfie. After all, an outstanding dating profile is useless without a topnotch photo, right?

Can love really be found on the Internet? Or is a real-world connection closer to Parker than he thinks?

Opportunity Knocks (Laissez Faire #1)

Small-town security guard, Gill Martin, has lived in Mystique Pointe his entire life. His dating prospects are non-existent and he doesn't particularly like his job, but at least it's better than unemployment. Besides, he hasn't got any better ideas.

Big-city artist, Tommy Hearne, knows exactly what he wants out of life: a successful art career and a successful relationship. He also knows that living in Liberty City is his best chance for pursuing both. Unfortunately, for him, neither of these pursuits seem to be panning out quite to his liking.

When Tommy and his misfit band of friends roll into town for the Laissez Faire, Mystique Pointe's annual music & art festival, worlds definitely collide. A fiery tryst sparks more than just a lust connection, but what happens when the weekend is over?

Judging A Book By Its Cover

Agonizingly shy Emory North has his life mapped out for him: finish his business degree, go to work for his father, and one day take over as CEO of North Star Publishing. More at home amongst stacks of books, Emory has little to no interest in his lot as 'North Jr.', but has never had the courage to follow his true passion—writing.

Brash and ballsy Bryce Palmer, editor-in-chief of ECLIPSE magazine is known for bedding and discarding PAs like yesterday's newspaper. He's up against a serious deadline and down two staff members. And the last thing he has time for is babysitting the spoiled rich son of a CEO. But when Pierce Barclay North insists now is the time for his heir apparent to get his feet wet in the company waters, Palmer's hands are tied.

But looks can be deceiving. And, sometimes, passion can spark in the most unlikely of places…

ANTHOLOGIES

Owned By The Alpha: Manlove Edition
Bad Alpha: Manlove Edition
Uniform Fetish: Manlove Edition

www.evernightpublishing.com